# DEATH WON: A NOVELLA

## By

## C.L. Sweatt

For
Jonathan
With
Love

Death Won

# Chapter 1

She watched the mourners walk by slowly and deliberately, intentionally controlling their paces to either not seem too anxious or walk too slowly, impeding the mourning of those who followed. From the corner of her eyes she caught a woman adjusting her stockings quickly before she got to the casket. All of these distractions provided temporary relief from the agonizing pain she felt in her heart. From the warm summer day they met, Dylan and Toni had been the best of friends. Burying her only friend seemed unfair and left a void in her life she'd never known before. Dylan's body was empty and blank, the opposite of the warm smiling man she'd met. A chord from the funeral home organ cut into Toni's thoughts, as the funeral went on and the last row made its way.

She intentionally sat as close to Dylan as she could and as the family would allow. Each step Toni took was with a tear. At twenty-one, it just was not right; they should be playing basketball or talking on the phone, anything but this.

Toni stood in front of her friend's body, awkward and alone. She stood there, needing a familiar hand holding hers, a friend to be her rock. She looked at the lifeless brownish gray skin as if looking for any signs of life. Toni's eyes were looking at a body but her mind was seeing a memory. His lips were reminders of a laugh, his nose broken from an accident, his eyes warm and caring. Oblivious to time, Toni did not hear the funeral director ask her if she was okay. She was looking at his hair, the neatly braided rows she had done the night before. Dylan would never let anyone but Toni braid his hair.

The hand of the funeral director slid away from Toni's upper arm, as she headed off to conclude the services. This was not how their story was supposed to end. Was this why she and Dylan had never talked about the future or the past? Because there would be neither; their lives would change in the blink of an eye.

After the funeral, Toni went home and sat on her couch. Needing someone to call for comfort and reassurance, Toni picked up the phone and dialed her mother, reluctant to speak of death. A recent doctor's visit revealed that her mom Charlene was dying from stage 3 breast cancer. It was an unexpected revelation from such a religious, faith filled woman. Toni did her best to accommodate her mother's condition, and as a twenty-one year-old finding her way, was not coping well. After a brief conversation with Charlene, Toni sadly ended the phone call and retreated to the sofa, still warm and inviting. Charlene, having just completed chemotherapy the day before, was incoherent and barely able to hold the phone. The loss of her friend and the loss of the strong, resilient mother she once knew were too much for Toni to bear. Charlene had been reduced by her cancer to one third of her size and none of her strength. Charlene had lost all of her beautiful coal black curly hair in clumps one Sunday afternoon.

While Toni sat and reflected over the last six months, she felt a growing desperation to get up and get out. Hailing a taxi to the city or just taking the trash out would suffice. The child growing inside of her was a constant reminder that there were things to look forward to despite the chaos and loss around her. Her pregnancy was a surprise and she was planning to give the baby to an adoptive family. In a fit of anger and denial, Toni had disappeared from her boyfriend's life without telling him that she was expecting. She had always been careful and despite her boyfriend's pleas, she did not want to have any children. Toni had grown suspicious when her boyfriend suddenly began asking her strange questions. One day he asked her what she would do if she accidentally got pregnant. That day,

Toni packed up her things she kept at his apartment and just left. Since Charlene's prognosis and Dylan's death Toni began having second thoughts about the adoption. Even though she had already contacted the selected adoptive parents to let them know she had changed her mind, she was not ready to face her fear of becoming a parent.

# Chapter 2

It was 3:02 A.M. when Toni suddenly awakened from a deep, much needed sleep. The light from the street lamp outside her bedroom window softly illuminated the small, quiet room. The periodic stirring from sleep in to an alert state was typical during the first trimester but this time it was different. Toni became frightened, realizing that she was not alone in the room. Too scared to move, she lay still listening and waiting.

It was now 3:53 A.M. and Toni still lay frozen in place, tears streaming into her pillow. After the disappointment of the last few weeks, her life boiled down to being pregnant alone and possibly murdered. The urge to go pee finally became so unbearable Toni sprang up from her bed and ran to the bathroom door four feet from the bed. In one motion, she swung open the door and closed it behind her, and pushed in the lock without looking into the bedroom. Panting hard with her back against the door, Toni pressed her ear against the cool white paint and listened for footsteps. There were no sounds coming from the bedroom. When Toni was too tired to be scared, she slowly turned the door knob and pushed open the door. The door swung open and bounced off the window sill. The room was still, undisturbed and no one was there. This was the third time this had happened in the last three days and it was taking its toll. The lack of sleep had Toni feeling like a zombie and she began to question whether or not she was actually losing her mind. Other strange things had been happening that could not be answered. Two days prior, after returning home from a long morning working on her job at a local radio station, Toni opened the front door to find her shoes in the middle of the floor in the hallway at the threshold of the living room. It was strange and frightening but Toni concluded that it was her forgetfulness that came with being pregnant. The first day of the strange occurrences was the most prominent in her mind. She was showering the morning of Dylan's funeral and the power in her apartment shut off for one minute and her lights flickered and then everything came back on. In her four years living in her downtown apartment, she'd never had any issues with the power. Even during the cold Michigan winters when ice clung to the power lines, there had been no problems with the electricity.

Two weeks had passed after Toni's three days of terror and sleeplessness only to begin again. Her mother's condition was deteriorating to the point where she was placed on hospice and given three months to live. Toni visited her mother as much as she could. Having no friends or close family left Toni plenty of time to focus on her mother's well being and preparing for the birth of her new baby. One afternoon, while walking to the hospice center a few miles away, something interesting happened. There was a little delicatessen that served the locals. Toni loved to disappear in this little place, away in a corner facing the busy street. Finding comfort in a warm Reuben sandwich and cheese Danish was a treat for her. On this particular day around noon, the deli was packed full of businessmen, doctors, and hospital staff all bustling about rushing to get their lunches and get back to work. Toni, wearing a summer dress and sandals, well into her second trimester and obviously pregnant at first glance, waited patiently in line. She stood looking over the different pastries, searching for a reason to try something different. When it was time to check out, that mission was a bust and she requested her regular order after being greeted by the store manager.

Toni did not notice the man in a dark gray Armani suit watching her. He watched the pregnant woman get her lunch as he debated within himself on whether or not to speak to her. He could not help but observe the sadness in her beautiful brown eyes. He finished his lunch while watching her closely, then reached into his pocket and felt around for the silver dollar he'd kept for good luck. It was a gift from his father when he graduated from the university. It had served him well and the sadness in Toni's eyes warranted him to want that for her. Just as he'd began focusing on the content of his pockets, he saw the beautiful yet sad stranger gathering her things to leave. He stopped her and said, "Excuse me, miss."

Toni looked up, startled by the handsome stranger standing in front of her. She felt less threatened as she looked into his kind eyes and at his salt-and-pepper hair. He placed in her palm the silver dollar and told her to put it into her baby's piggy bank. A confused and grateful Toni told the gentleman thank you, and as soon as he'd appeared in front of her, he'd blended into the crowd of new patrons entering the deli. Toni hastily left the deli and began heading toward her mother's hospice.

The hospice staff greeted Toni as she signed in and began the long trek to Charlene's room. Tired from her two mile walk, Toni shuffled along the hospice corridor, observing the bingo game going on in the cafeteria, the freshly potted flowers on a console table in the hall. Toni knew Charlene was not playing bingo. Charlene's room was on the first floor at the end of the east wing near an emergency exit. Charlene's sisters had taken the time to paint her room a rose petal pink to make it more comfortable. Toni entered her mother's dimly lit room as the hospice nurse was leaving. They exchanged solemn glances as a little bit of hope drained from both of their eyes. Toni took her seat by the hospital bed while Charlene quietly slept. She was careful not to wake the woman in front of her who loved and nurtured Toni until their roles were switched. Toni reflected on the last year: giving Charlene shots after chemotherapy, the nausea and the vomiting, the late night cries. Charlene began to wake up from her sleep and Toni rushed to choke back tears and grabbed Charlene's hand.

Once Charlene realized someone was there, she woke up to see her baby girl smiling and holding her hand. On the way out, the nurse told Toni that Charlene was not eating and had no appetite. Toni asked Charlene why she was not eating and Charlene told Toni that she was hungry. Toni stood up and asked Charlene what she wanted to eat. "A chicken," Charlene replied. Toni was not sure, so she asked again. "A chicken," Charlene repeated. Toni kissed her mother on the forehead and set off to find a chicken.

Toni was determined, confused, and a little irritated that Charlene could not want something that was readily available, but thinking about all that Charlene had gone through in the last year made those thoughts insignificant. Toni walked to the nearest grocery store and picked the biggest, juiciest rotisserie chicken out of the deli window. The grocery was closer to Toni's house than it was to the hospice, but none of that mattered. Toni returned to Charlene's hospice room and placed the chicken on Charlene's hospital tray. There was no hesitation. Charlene went in; she knew what she wanted, sick or not. Toni was tired and did not want to get caught by the setting sun, so she kissed her precious mother on the forehead and began the two-mile walk toward home.

# Chapter 3

Toni began her regular routine of looking in the refrigerator, looking out of the window, looking at the clock, channel surfing, then finally retreating to her room for the night. Feeling the weight of the day in her mind body and soul fade away, Toni was startled by the feeling of someone sitting behind her on the opposite side of her bed. No one was there. She knew no one was there, but she knew that she felt the bed sink down behind her. This happened before—the night before Charlene went to hospice, and this time it was not the same; it was no longer frightening. Toni felt her being open up to whatever was happening around her as she drifted off to sleep.


Toni awoke to find herself standing in a room with a clock large enough to fill an entire wall. The clock was spinning as if it were being fast-forwarded by some invisible hand at the speed of light. It suddenly stopped exactly on 3:02. Toni recognized this time from somewhere. It was the time she woke up for three nights. It was the time Dylan supposedly died. Toni heard arguing in the background and turned to see Dylan with his back to her in another room. Just as she got his name in her mouth, a gunshot rang out and everything froze in time. Dylan, the clock, his name in her mouth, the sound of the shot, rang like a bell in her ears. The clock shattered into thousands of tiny pieces and flew toward Toni's face.

Toni sat straight up in bed, gasping for air. She reached onto the bedside table, knocking over a glass of water before finding the lamp switch. Confused by the dream she'd just had, Toni reminded herself that Dylan had killed himself and was alone in the house when he died. At least that is what the police detective had told her.

They were supposed to be going to a movie together the day Dylan died. The decision to go to the movies came months after meeting on a breezy summer day the year before. Toni was getting the brakes fixed on an old '76 Monte Carlo she'd gotten from an auction. As a busy college student, it was a dependable yet inexpensive ride. It lasted 6 months before her $150 investment was gone when the engine died. Toni was sitting in the waiting area thumbing through books when Dylan and his friend Paul walked in, laughing and full of life. They briefly caught Toni's attention but she turned back to the low-rider magazine in her hands. After about five minutes, Dylan approached Toni. "What do you know about low-riders?" Toni responded by rolling her eyes and pointing to the sparkly blue and gold 1978 Monte Carlo on the garage lift. Dylan's eyebrows raised and they began talking about whatever came to mind. The mechanic called from behind the counter, letting Toni know that it would be another hour. Feeling restless, Toni decided to walk half a mile across the Fall Way Bridge to the record store and get some records. While working part time at the local radio station, Toni learned the art of Dee Jing and enjoyed it quite a bit. When she ended her conversation with Dylan and stood to leave, he asked her where she was going. She told him and he refused to let her walk alone.

When Toni, Dylan, and Paul arrived at the record store they all went in different directions. Toni headed to the vinyl albums and singles, Dylan to the Compact discs and Paul to the discounted old cassette tapes. Toni's favorite song came on the loud speaker in the record store and she lifted her head just in time to see a big smile on Dylan's face. The old Motown hit was his favorite too. They sang it together and danced happily as they stood in line. Paul chimed in with the few words he knew and they all sang as if they were the only ones in the store. Something magical happened in that moment. They laughed all the way back to the mechanics shop like they had known each other for years. When they reached their final destination Toni and Dylan exchanged phone numbers and vowed to stay in touch. Every day since the day they met, Toni and Dylan talked on the phone. Dylan shared his quests on his computer game Dungeons and Dragons and Toni talked about her new mixes and school. They never spoke of the past and never thought of the future. Their friendship was unique in a time full of expectations and demands. They demanded nothing of each other and expected even less. They shared one common interest: talking to each other on the phone. One Saturday evening, Toni and Dylan made plans to catch a movie at the cinema the following day. Just as they had spoken on the phone so many times before, the plans they made were set in stone.

There was nothing special about that Sunday morning. Around noon, Toni found herself watching the clock. She decided it would be best if she completed her laundry to make the time go by a little bit faster. Dylan said he would call and get her address and try to head over around 2:30 P.M. Two-thirty came and went, and Toni began to feel let down. At 2:57 PM, Toni went down stairs to put her last load of laundry in to the dryer. Once the clothes were in the dryer with the door closed, Toni turned to head up the stairs only to be stopped dead in her tracks by an overwhelming feeling of grief and panic. She placed her hands over her chest and stepped backward away from the stairs before collapsing on a bench at the foot of the staircase against the wall. Toni began shaking and crying for reasons she didn't know. She did not understand what was happening or why she felt this paralyzing feeling of fear and a grief worse than she had ever experienced before. Feeling uncertain and frightened by what had just occurred, Toni ran up the stairs back to her apartment to get her phone. There were no missed calls and it was now 3:03 P.M.

Toni tried to call Dylan several times Sunday evening but there was no answer. Monday after her first course was over, Toni rushed to the payphone in the campus commons area only to find a long line. Her next class was starting soon and she didn't have time to wait. Instead, she rushed back to the open payphone during lunchtime. Fumbling to place the change into the slots, Toni dialed Dylan's number for the first time on Monday. A woman answered the phone; Toni recognized the voice as Dylan's sister Tonya. After asking for Dylan, there was a long pause. Tonya told Toni that Dylan was gone; he was in Heaven. After offering condolences, Toni hung up the phone in shock.

Later that evening, Tonya called Toni and explained that Dylan had committed suicide Sunday afternoon. Toni immediately replayed the scene that took place in the basement of her building while doing laundry. Could she have really experienced some sort of supernatural occurrence at the time of Dylan's death? Heartbroken and confused, she could not believe that her friend was dead. "We had plans," Toni thought to herself. It just did not make sense and she had to get to the bottom of it.

For several days, Toni contacted the police department to find the detective overseeing the death investigation. The day before Dylan's funeral, Detective Robert Stein finally returned Toni's calls. Detective Stein patiently answered Toni's questions before explaining the events leading to Dylan's death. According to Detective Stein's account, Dylan and Paul were preparing to leave when Dylan stated that he had forgotten something and went back into the house. Paul was outside when he heard a gunshot. Paul ran into the house to find out what happened and found his friend dying on the bedroom floor. Toni explained to the detective that the story did not make sense and Dylan never showed any suicidal tendencies. Toni explained their friendship to the detective, though it seemed to fall on to deaf ears. The detective was convinced that Toni's friend Dylan had committed suicide, case closed. Detective Stein explained to Toni that according to Dylan's friends and family, Dylan had been suicidal for the last year. Just over the last couple of months before his death, Dylan stopped talking about suicide. Detective Stein told Toni that usually when suicidal people stop talking about suicide, it is because they have already made up their minds to proceed.

This revelation hit Toni like a ton of bricks; she slowly dropped to her knees in the center of her room. Toni did not know what to think about the new information. She assumed that maybe a suicidal person stops talking about suicide because they changed their mind.

# Chapter 4

Toni began to realize that on her most emotionally charged days, her visitor would sit on her bed until she fell asleep. It was a welcoming comfort amidst the pain and turmoil. Charlene's heartbeat was not as strong these days and the conversations were growing shorter and shorter. This, compounded with Dylan's death, was too much for a lone soul to handle. Toni continued having the same dream with the sound of Dylan arguing followed by the gunshot. Toni was beginning to believe that Dylan's death was not a suicide but a murder, and she was going to find out the truth.

The investigation consumed every part of Toni's life outside of school and work. She had spent so much time at the police station questioning investigators that they knew her by name and even shared their doughnuts. After one particular conversation, Detective Stein reassured Toni that he would take another look at the case and keep her posted.

Summer ended and fall came and went. Charlene lingered between life and death for months until the day before Thanksgiving, when Charlene took her last breath. The day Charlene had passed was a bitterly cold day. Toni's walk to the hospice seemed a little longer and the deli was closed. The leaves had all fallen from the trees and the world seemed colorless, cold, and alone. It was difficult for Toni to find any beauty in that cold November day.

The nurses had called the family early that day and told them to come to the hospice to say their last goodbyes. Toni and her family members perched at Charlene's bedside in waves. A room was set up down the hall for family members to rest and gather themselves throughout the night into the morning. Toni sat at Charlene's side until her body could no longer handle sitting in the chair. Toni would then switch chairs, always keeping a hand on Charlene, letting her know that she was there. Toni sat bowed at the foot of Charlene's bed, holding her feet in her hands. Charlene could not speak, but she wiggled her toes, letting Toni know she was there.

When the responses became fewer throughout the night and into the morning, Toni decided to get an hour's rest in the little room down the hall. With her mind, body, and soul exhausted, Toni lay down and closed her eyes when a gentle hand touched her shoulder. Charlene had taken her last breath.

Sobbing deep into her pillow, Toni felt her heart explode in her chest. There was no Thanksgiving for Toni that year; only sadness.

# Chapter 5

The day of Charlene's funeral was the day that would change Toni's life forever.


Toni rose early on the day of her mother's burial. The visitor who sat on her bed was no longer invisible or alone. There sat Dylan and Charlene at the foot of Toni's bed. Dylan looked exactly as he did the day they'd met. Charlene looked years younger and more beautiful than Toni had ever seen her. Her beautiful brown skin was glowing and radiant. Too defeated to be scared, Toni's heart asked why. She suddenly saw the familiar dream playing in her mind's eye. Paul's face was the stranger arguing with Dylan before his death. The voices were now clear and distinct. Paul and Dylan were arguing over Dylan's gun. Dylan had the gun pointing to his own chin. Paul was attempting to tell Dylan that he had so much to look forward to and that Toni was waiting on him. Dylan told Paul that he knew, but he had already ruined it. Paul asked Dylan why and he replied, "I never told Toni that I have children. The whole time I have been so scared of losing our friendship by telling her. She does not have any children yet and she is scared of being a parent. It will never work." Dylan pulled the trigger and a shot rang out, Toni gasped for air; Dylan's body fell to the floor. Paul, in shock, and scared that he would be blamed, told the police that Dylan returned to the house after they had left and shot himself. Toni looked into the regretful face of Dylan's spirit as it vanished into a mist right before her eyes. Charlene knowingly smiled and faded into a brilliantly colorful mist that swirled around the room like a vortex. There were colors without names all around, embracing Toni with love and a peace that she'd never felt before.

Charlene's funeral was a ritual for those who may not have known what Toni knew in her heart. The body in the casket was nothing compared to what once was and what now is. It was a mere shell, a reminder of an existence extended.

www.ingramcontent.com/pod-product-compliance
Lightning Source LLC
Chambersburg PA
CBHW050918120626
46552CB00004B/1633